W9-BAN-203

PUFFIN BOOKS

Aussie Nibbles

First Friend

It is Kerry's first day at her new
school. Will she find a friend?
But why does the big black dog
follow her around?

which Aussie Nibbles have you read?

Aussie Nibbles

First Friend

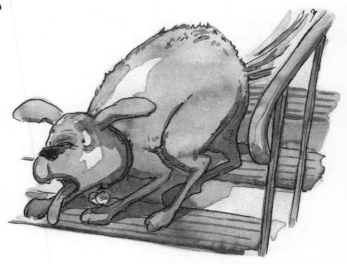

Christobel Mattingley

Illustrated by Craig Smith

Puffin Books

Puffin Books

Penguin Group (Australia)
250 Camberwell Road
Camberwell, Victoria 3124, Australia
Penguin Books Ltd
80 Strand, London WC2R 0RL, England
Penguin Group (USA) Inc.
375 Hudson Street, New York, New York 10014, USA
Penguin Books, a division of Pearson Canada
10 Alcorn Avenue, Toronto, Ontario, Canada, M4V 3B2
Penguin Books (N.Z.) Ltd
Cnr Rosedale and Airborne Roads, Albany, Auckland, New Zealand
Penguin Books (South Africa) (Pty) Ltd
24 Sturdee Avenue, Rosebank, Johannesburg 2196, South Africa
Penguin Books India (P) Ltd
11, Community Centre, Panchsheel Park, New Delhi 110 017, India

First published as *Black Dog* by Collins, 1981
This revised edition first published by Penguin Books Australia, 2000

9 11 13 15 17 19 20 18 16 14 12 10

Copyright © Christobel Mattingley, 2000
Illustrations copyright © Craig Smith, 2000

The moral right of the author and illustrator has been asserted

All rights reserved. Without limiting the rights under copyright
reserved above, no part of this publication may be reproduced,
stored in or introduced into a retrieval system, or transmitted,
in any form or by any means (electronic, mechanical, photocopying,
recording or otherwise), without the prior written permission
of both the copyright owner and the above publisher of this book.

Typeset in New Century School Book by Post Pre-press Group,
Brisbane, Queensland
Printed in Australia by McPherson's Printing Group,
Maryborough, Australia

Designed by Melissa Fraser, Penguin Design Studio
Series editor: Kay Ronai

National Library of Australia
Cataloguing-in-Publication data:
Mattingley, Christobel, 1931– .
First friend.
ISBN 0 14 130894 X.
I. Smith, 1955– . II. Title. (Series: Aussie bites). (Series: Aussie nibbles).
A823.3

www.puffin.com.au

For David, my first friend. *C.M.*

For Casey Russell. *C.S.*

1
New School

Kerry had been to school for two terms. She had made many friends. She liked her teacher. And she had learned to read.

Then Kerry's father
changed his job.

Kerry's family moved to
another town, and Kerry
had to go to a different
school.

It was a much bigger
school. It was three storeys
high. There were many
flights of stairs and long
passages with dozens of
doors.

In Kerry's first school
there were twenty children
in her year. In the new
school there were one
hundred about Kerry's age.
There were four first

classes called by the points
of the compass: North,
South, East, West. Kerry
was in South.

Kerry's new teacher said,
'I am Miss Bell.' She was

short. Her hair was grey.
Kerry's other teacher had
been tall with golden hair
almost to her waist.

Miss Bell said, 'This is

Kerry, everyone.'

The other children smiled
at her, but their faces were
strange to her.

Kerry had always shared

a table with friends. But
now she had one all to
herself. At her old school
the tables had been
arranged in groups. Here
they were arranged in two

horseshoes, one inside the
other.

First of all they sang
songs. Miss Bell played the
music. There was a vase of
cheerful daffodils on the

shelf by the keyboard.

In Kerry's first school
there had been a bowl on
the cassette cupboard, and

the class had planted
daffodil bulbs in it. Kerry
wondered if they were
flowering yet.

Kerry did not know any
of the songs. At the end

Miss Bell said, 'Teach us
one of your songs, Kerry.'

But Kerry shook her
head.

'Tomorrow perhaps,'

smiled Miss Bell kindly.

Next they did maths.

Miss Bell gave Kerry a box

of counters, red, yellow,

green, all for herself.

'At my school we shared cubes,' Kerry said.

'We do it this way, by ourselves,' the children said.

Then Miss Bell said, 'You may go to the library now.'

2
A Long Way

The children hurried out
of the door, down the long
passage to the right.

They went across the
landing to the left, ran

down the stairs and across
another landing. They
passed an open door.

Kerry could see the
playground outside. But the
others went on down some

more stairs.

They jumped the two bottom steps.

To the right and straight ahead were two more doors to the playground. But the

children ran round the
corner to the left.

To Kerry it seemed a very
long way.

There were some more
doors with the sound of

recorders coming from
them. There was one door
with a sound of computers.

The children disappeared
through a quiet door.

Kerry followed.

3
Old Friends

A lady smiled at Kerry and
said, 'I am Mrs May, the
librarian. This is your first
day, isn't it?'

'My first day here,' said
Kerry. 'But I've been to
school before, of course.'

'Of course,' said Mrs May.
'Do you like reading?'

'Of course,' said Kerry.

'Then come here often to
read and change your
books. And you may borrow
books to take home

whenever you like. We keep

your bar code at this desk.'

'Thank you,' said Kerry.

She looked around the

room. It was much bigger

than the library at her old school. All around the walls there were shelves and shelves of books. Many more books than in her old school library.

There were books about
trains and tortoises, horses
and helicopters, dinosaurs
and dolphins, mice and
mountains.

There were books on how
to make things. There were
books on how to do things.
Kerry thought that there
must be a book on every
subject under the sun.

Then on a low shelf
beside a big red rug Kerry
saw all her favourite books.
*Where the Wild Things
Are* and *Winnie the Pooh*,
Peter Rabbit and *Willy*,

Corduroy and *The Rainbow
Fish, Babar* and *Each
Peach Pear Plum* were all
there.

*The Very Hungry
Caterpillar* was there. And

so were *Madeline* and *Ping*.

Kerry was among friends
again. She gathered them
into her arms and sat down
on the red rug.

The only books she left on
the shelf were *Arthur, Spot,
Hairy Maclary* and *Harry
the Dirty Dog*. Kerry did
not like dogs.

The other children chose
their books. Mrs May
waved her wand over their
bar codes. They put their
books in their bags.

A bell rang, but Kerry did not hear it.

'Goodbye,' said Mrs May. 'It's time for you to go. Come back soon.'

The other children left.

But Kerry lay on the red rug with her friends.

No one knew she was there.

4
Which Way?

Mrs May came to put away
some books. She found
Kerry. 'Still here! It's time
you went.'

Kerry stood up slowly.

It was hard to leave her
friends.

'You may take one with
you,' Mrs May said.

It was hard to choose.

'What about *Arthur* or
Harry?' said Mrs May.

Kerry shook her head.
She did not like dogs.

'Do you know the way
back?'

Kerry nodded.

But outside the library
door she stopped.

The passage went left. It
went right. It stretched
long and empty, empty of
people but full of sound.

There were sounds of
recorders from behind the
doors where people played.
There were sounds of
computers behind the door

where people surfed.

At both ends there were
doors with glimpses of
grass and trees.

Kerry turned left.

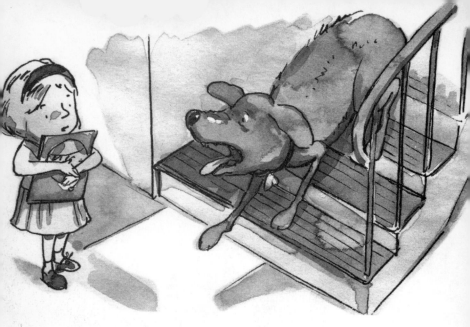

In the distance she could
see stairs going up. She
walked to the stairs.

A big black dog bounded
down the stairs.

Kerry stopped and stood
still. She did not like dogs.

5
Black Dog

The black dog jumped
the two bottom steps. It
bounded up to Kerry.

Kerry stood very still.
She could feel its hot

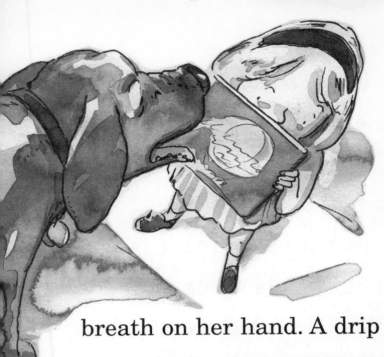

breath on her hand. A drip
from its mouth dropped on
her shiny black shoe.

She darted to the stairs.
The black dog jumped in
her way, in the middle of
the stairs.

Kerry tried to hurry to one side.

The black dog barked and moved in front of her.

Kerry moved to the other side. The black dog moved

too. It moved the same way.

Kerry turned around. She hurried back down the long passage.

The black dog followed.

Kerry came to another

flight of stairs. The black
dog passed her. It started to
walk up the stairs, its tail
waving like a flag.

Kerry heard footsteps
echo down the passage.

She looked around. Mrs
May was walking away to
the other end.

Kerry turned back. She
ran as quickly as she could,
as quietly as she could,

after Mrs May.

She reached the bottom
of the stairs.

Mrs May had gone. But
the black dog was there
again, on the second step.

Kerry said, 'Go away, dog.'

Her voice was swallowed by

the stair well.

The black dog barked.

Kerry turned and ran.

The black dog was at her
heels. As she reached the
other stairs the black dog
bounded past.

6
New Friend

Miss Bell was coming down the stairs.

'I thought you might be lost. It's such a big school, so many storeys and so

many stairs, such long
passages and so many
doors,' she said.

'But Black Dog has found
you.' She patted the black
dog.

Kerry said, 'He barked at me. He stopped me going up the stairs.'

Miss Bell said, 'He knew they were not the right stairs. He knew you had lost your way.'

Kerry asked, 'Is he your dog?'

'Yes,' Miss Bell smiled.

'Of course he should not be at school. But he is always so lonely at home by himself on the first day

after the holidays.' She
patted him again.

'He follows me to school.
He likes looking after

children on their first day.
He likes making new
friends.'

'He is my first friend
here,' Kerry said. She
patted his back very lightly,
very quickly.

Black Dog wagged his
tail.

'He is my first dog friend.'

'It is playtime now,' Miss
Bell said. 'Black Dog will

take you outside. He will
show you where the other
children are playing.'

Black Dog bounded up
the stairs. Kerry followed.

Together they went out the
door to the playground.

Black Dog and Kerry ran
across the grass.

'Hello, Kerry! Hello, Black

Dog!' the children called.

'Come and play with us.'

They all joined in a game together.

From Christobel Mattingley

The idea for this story came when
I worked in a school where the
library was in the basement.

One day a little new girl arrived.
At the end of her first library lesson
she didn't leave with the others.
After I sent her off to her classroom,
I wondered if she knew the way.
So I went to check and found her
on the stairs with a dog.

When I was her age I'd been scared
of dogs too, so I knew how she felt.
Now I love dogs and have many dog
friends.

From Craig Smith

I have always had cats. Once I had three cats and twelve kittens!

Dogs scared me a bit until I met my neighbour's dog. It's part Labrador, part something else. We're not sure. He visits me often, and sits outside my window while I draw.

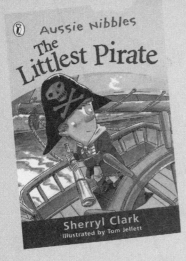

Nicholas Nosh is the littlest pirate in the world. His family won't let him go to sea and he's bored. 'I'll show them,' he says.

What happens when Cinderfella, of the Planet Jetsonia, meets Princess Esmerelda of the Planet Earth?

Crystal longs to be a mermaid. So her mother makes her a special tail.

Benny loves the dog that lives nearby. But why is it so sad?

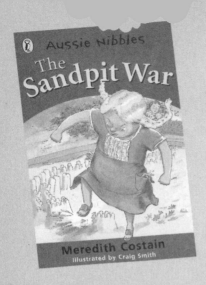

Four friends. Best friends forever.
Then along came Eartha and the
sandpit war . . .

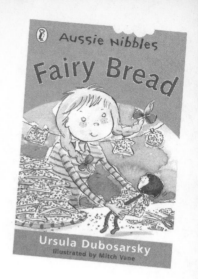

Becky only wants fairy bread at
her party. But there's so much left
over, and she won't throw it out.

Daryl, the baby magpie,
has to find his own food.
But how?

Their grandmother loved blue.
She also hated her grey hair.
Sonya and Margo knew what to do